To Thomas and Connor,
Enjoy all your celebrations.

from
Simone
(your cousin's grandma)

To Bella, Max, Maddy, Hailey, Lucca,
James, Julian, Ava, and "expected."
–S. N.

To my whole extended family and all of the
quirky things that became our traditions.
–B. B.

ISBN 13: 978-1-59298-935-5

Library of Congress Catalog Number: 2014905319
Printed in the United States of America
First Printing: 2014
18 17 16 15 14   5 4 3 2 1

Cover and interior design by Brian Barber

BEAVER'S POND
PRESS

Beaver's Pond Press, Inc.
7108 Ohms Lane
Edina, MN 55439-2129
(952) 829-8818
www.BeaversPondPress.com

To order, visit www.BeaversPondBooks.com or call 1-800-901-3480. Reseller discounts available.

Eight Candles and a Tree

By Simone Bloom Nathan

Illustrations by Brian Barber

crunch
swoosh

went the tree into Sophie's house.
Tommy had a tree, too.

twinkle sparkle

glowed the lights on the bushes in Sophie's yard.

Tommy had yard lights, too.

shimmer flicker

burned the candles
of the menorah in Sophie's window.

Tommy didn't have a menorah.

mmmmmmmmm

came a wonderful smell
as soon as the door swung open.

SSSSsSs

crackled the latkes
frying in the pan.
Sophie's grandma spread
sizzling potato cakes
on paper towels to drain.

Sophie and Tommy set bowls of sour cream and applesauce next to another menorah.
"How many menorahs do you have?" asked Tommy.
"Just two," said Sophie.
"I chose this one, because it's so sparkly.
The one in the window was my great-great-grandma's, and my grandma gave it to us."

Sophie helped her mom
light candles in the menorah
and together they recited
a short Hebrew prayer.

Tommy spooned applesauce
onto his latke.

Yum!

"It's crunchy and salty and sweet all at once!
I could eat these every day.
Why do you only eat them on Hanukkah?"

"To remind us of a miracle that
happened long ago in Israel," said Sophie.

"Once, there was just enough oil
in the Temple to give light for one night,
but it burned for eight nights long.
That's why we light a candle
each night for eight nights,
and eat food made in oil, like latkes."

"That makes sense," said Tommy.
"But how does the Christmas tree fit in?"
"It doesn't," said Sophie.

"We have a tree because Dad is Christian, and we have menorahs because Mom is Jewish. Our family celebrates **BOTH** holidays."

"You're lucky!" said Tommy.
"We only celebrate Christmas.
What else do you do on Hanukkah?"

"Hanukkah is so much fun—what do you do for Christmas?" asked Tommy.

"First we decorate the tree,
then Dad runs his old train around the bottom.
We stay in pajamas all Christmas day,
and eat stacks and stacks of pancakes.
How about you?"

"First Grandpa reads the poem

'Twas the Night Before Christmas'

in his deepest, loudest voice.

Then Mom plays piano and we all sing carols.
Of course we open presents, and eat a big roast.
It's great, but it's not eight days long.
Which do you like better, Hanukkah or Christmas?"

"Oh, I love them **both!**" beamed Sophie.
"Both have lights, and songs,
and special food, and presents…"

"And what I like best is that we all celebrate **TOGETHER!**"